the girl who loved
WELLIES

for Zadie x

First published in 2012 by Macmillan Children's Books, a division of Macmillan
Publishers Limited, 20 New Wharf Road, London N1 9RR, Basingstoke and Oxford
Associated companies throughout the world www.panmacmillan.com
ISBN: 978-0-230-74857-6 (HB) ISBN: 978-0-230-74858-3 (PB)
Text and illustrations copyright © Zehra Hicks 2012.

Zehra Hicks

the girl who loved WELLIES

Macmillan Children's Books

Molly

loved

She loved them so much, she wore them all the time.

In the bath . . .

On the beach . . .

Even in bed.

She never took them off!

And no one could make
her wear anything else.

One day, Molly had a big itch right in between her toes.

just here

She tried to scratch it,
but she couldn't reach.

So she tried her umbrella . . .

and the vacuum cleaner.

Even the dog tried to help.

But the itch wouldn't go away.

There was only one
thing left to do . . .

take the wellies OFF!

Molly pulled . . .

and pulled . . .

and pulled.

EVERYBODY

PULLED!

Molly loved her new toes so much . . .

That now she only wears . . .

flip-flops!

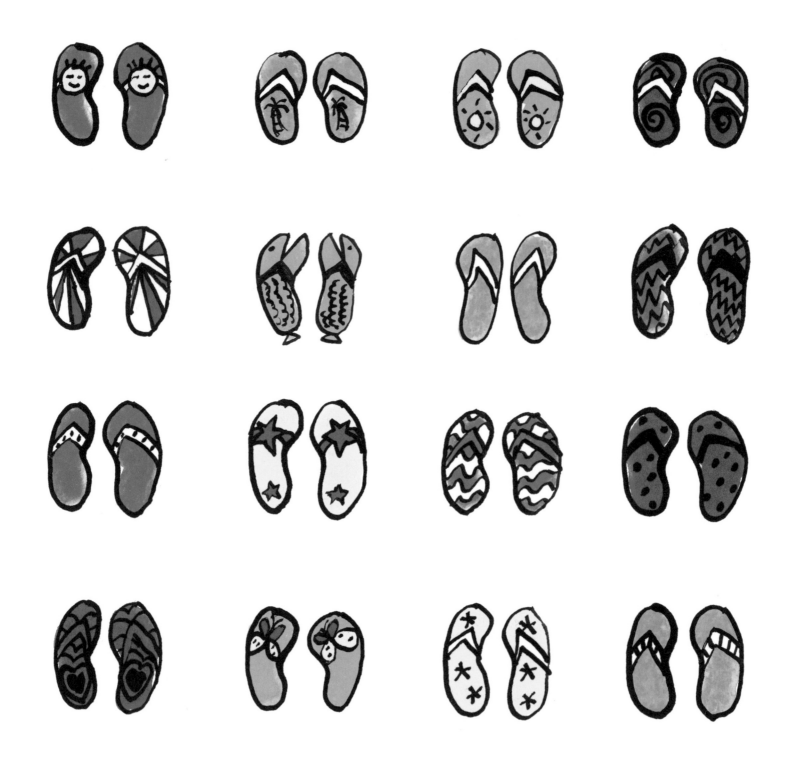

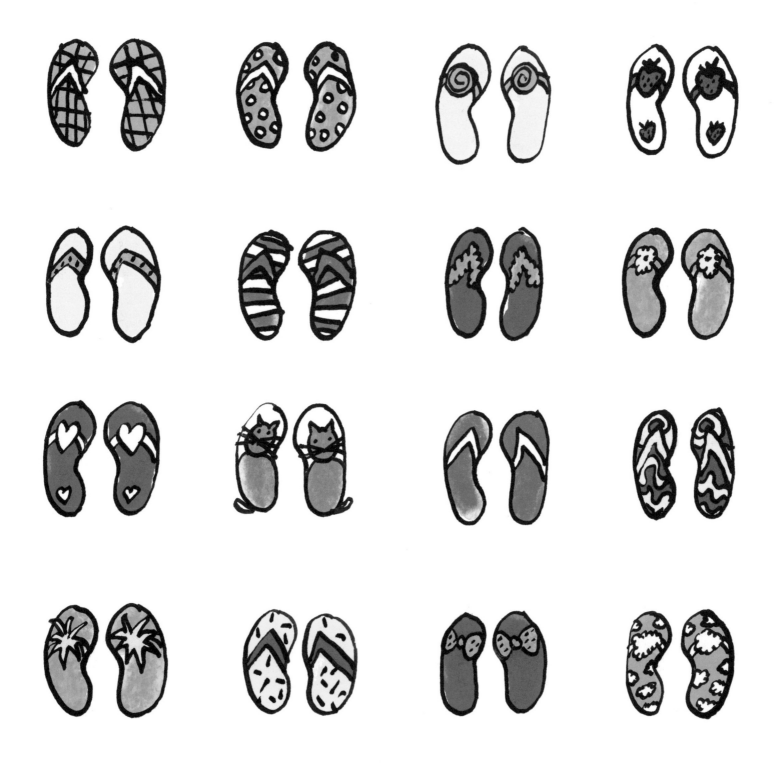